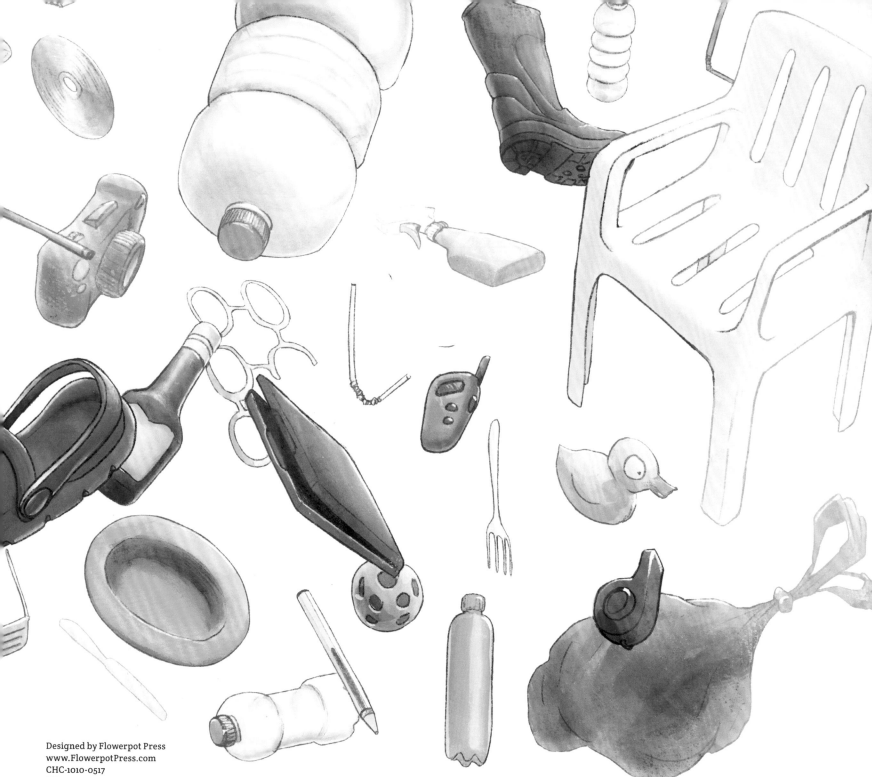

Designed by Flowerpot Press
www.FlowerpotPress.com
CHC-1010-0517
ISBN: 978-1-4867-2109-2
Made in China/Fabriqué en Chine

GRAMMY® AWARD-WINNING ARTIST

Keb' Mo'

with his friends

Colin Linden

and Chip Esten

DON'T THROW IT AWAY

Illustrated by Charlie Astrella

Hi there,

I'm Keb' Mo'. My friends, Colin and Charles, and I wrote a song called "Don't Throw It Away." Then we made it into this book, and I'm really glad you want to read it. A fun thing about this book also being a song is that you can listen to me sing it in a lot of places, and if you listen and turn the pages, it will be like I'm singing this book with you. Pretty cool, right?

Whether we sing it together or you read it on your own, I wanted to tell you a little about why we wrote it. We love this beautiful world and right now it could really use our help. We can all do a little bit (or a lot) to make things better. We can start by using less plastic. I know it is hard to use NO plastic, but if we think about it, we can use less. And that is a good thing. Every little bit helps. There are lots of ideas out there for how to do this. We even talk about some of them in the back of this book! People are thinking up new ways every day, and maybe you can too.

I hope when you read this book you decide to do a little bit to help. Maybe someday you can write your own song or book about helping the world and I hope that I get to hear it. Until then, remember it's a beautiful world, baby. Don't you throw it away!

Love,
Keb'

Who is Leo B.?

If you can believe it, there was once a time without plastic. The first big breakthrough in the world of plastic was in 1907 when Leo Baekeland created the first plastic that was made entirely out of synthetic materials, meaning that it was completely inorganic. Bakelite, as it was known, was a huge innovation, and it spawned what is often called "the age of plastics." Although Baekeland wasn't alive for most of the new forms of plastic, he never could have predicted what plastic would become and how it would affect our world today. When Leo Baekeland created his infamous invention, he was just trying to help make our lives easier.

Leo B. had a big idea!
Something that would last for a million years.

You see, someday we will all disappear,
but the big idea will still be here.

You've got to use it again.
Baby, don't you throw it away!

Now, who could imagine everything it would bring.
You can turn that plastic into any old thing.

It's so convenient, you just can't beat it,
'til it gets in the ocean and the fish start to eat it.

You've got to use it again.
Baby, don't you throw it away!

Well now, a turtle can't swim and a bird can't sing
when they're stuck in the hole of a six-pack ring.

We've got bottles and bags, caps and cups.
We've got too much stuff; we've got to clean it all up!

You've got to use it again.
Baby, don't you throw it away!

Well, the face of this planet, as far as I can see,
it could use just a little plastic surgery.

Leo didn't know he was starting a mess.
How it all turns out is anyone's guess.

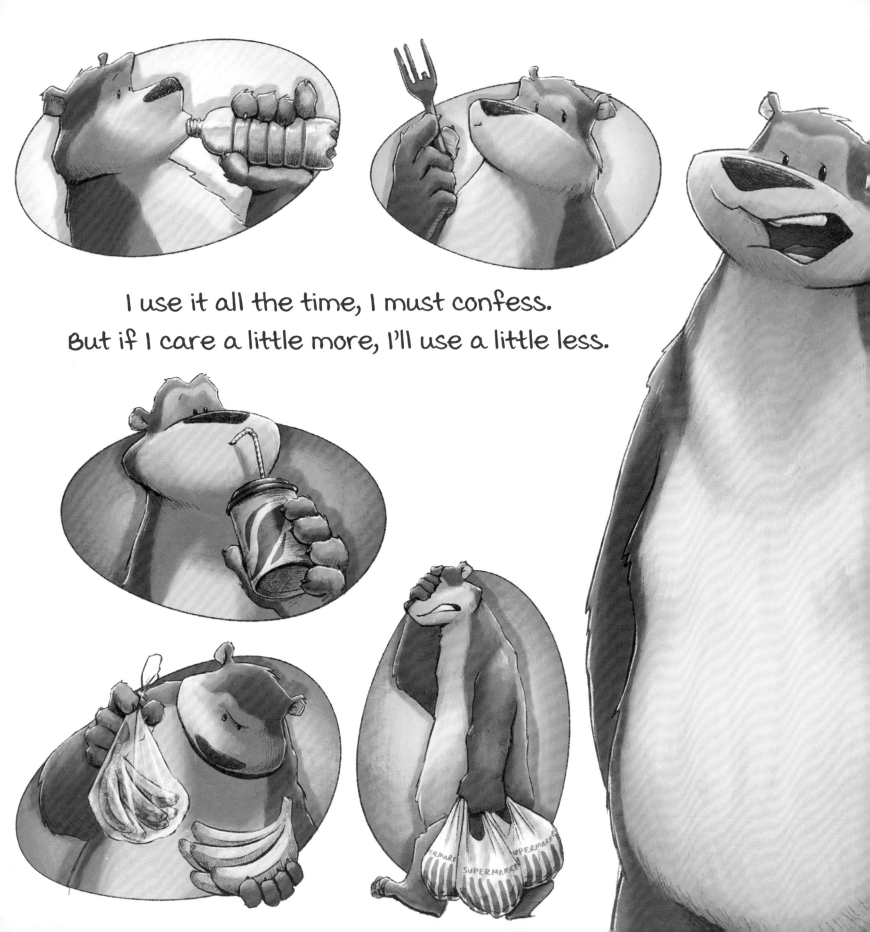

I use it all the time, I must confess.
But if I care a little more, I'll use a little less.

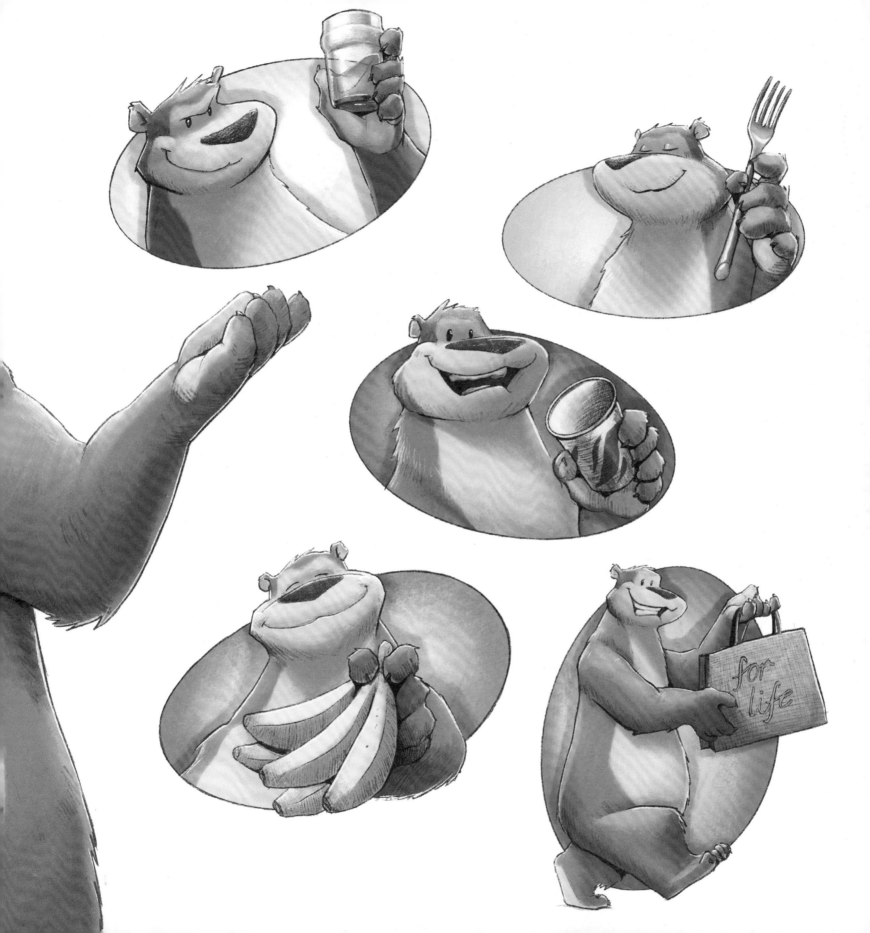

You've got to use it again.
Baby, don't you throw it away!

'Cause it's a beautiful world.
Baby, don't you throw it away.

There are so many ways that we can help protect our planet in our day-to-day lives beyond just recycling. Recycling is a good way to help out, but did you know that you can also reuse and even refuse? Discover more about the good, better, and best ways you can limit waste at home, at school, or anywhere you go!

DON'T THROW IT AWAY... It's good to recycle!

Recycling is the process of collecting certain items and processing them so they can be turned into something new. You can recycle all sorts of things, for example, cardboard, glass, paper, plastic, metal, clothes, and even some electronics. Generally, you can know if something can be recycled by checking for the recycling symbol on the item. Being mindful of what you put in the trash can help save energy and reduce pollution.

TIPS FOR RECYCLING:

Learn about how recycling is collected in your town. Sometimes it can be collected in blue bags and sometimes it needs to be sorted.

Try making recycling bins for your home. Decorate and label each one so you know where to collect your items.

Go out and collect recyclable items from your local park. Challenge your friends to see who can collect the most items!

Visit your local recycling center to learn more about how recycled items are processed.

YOU'VE GOT TO USE IT AGAIN... It's better to reuse!

Instead of throwing objects away, you can find lots of fun and creative ways to reuse them. Reusing items is a great way to support the environment and to use your creativity. There are some items called single-use items that should not be reused and should just be recycled or sometimes need to be thrown away. But there are plenty of other items that can be used in so many different ways!

TIPS FOR REUSING:

Try making a birdfeeder out of toilet paper rolls. Just cover it in peanut butter and birdseed and hang it in your yard.

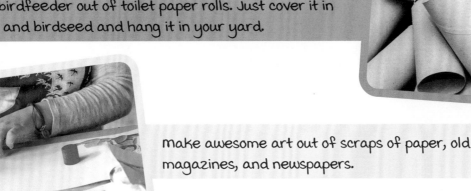

Make awesome art out of scraps of paper, old magazines, and newspapers.

Donate your old clothes and toys to a local donation center so they can be used again by someone else.

Organize a swap day with your friends. Bring items that you no longer use and trade them for items you may not already have.

Shop for items and clothing second-hand.

Borrow books from the library instead of buying brand new ones.

BUT IF I CARE A LITTLE MORE, I'LL USE A LITTLE LESS... It's best to refuse!

One of the best ways you can do your part to combat environmental waste is to do your best to refuse single-use items, such as plastic water bottles and plastic bags. It can be hard to refuse all the time but making an effort to refuse items can make a big difference in keeping our planet healthy.

TIPS FOR REFUSING:

Use reusable drinking straws instead of plastic straws.

Avoid single-use plastic water bottles and replace them with reusable water bottles instead.

Bring your own reusable silverware instead of using plastic spoons, knives, and forks.

Pack a waste-free lunch by using reusable containers instead of plastic bags.

Suggest walking or riding your bike to local places rather than riding in a car.

Turn down plastic bags when you shop. Instead bring your own tote bag from home.

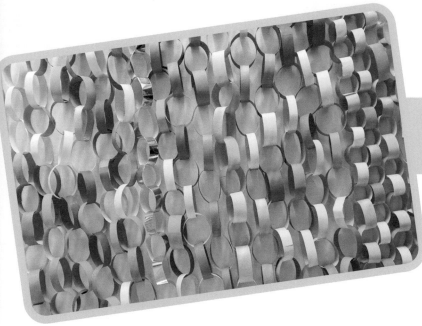

Don't use balloons as decorations for celebrations. Instead, make your own decorations with items you have at home.

Avoid individually wrapped snacks, such as chips or yogurt. Larger containers use less plastic than packs of individual items and can sometimes be reused.

Award-winning singer, songwriter, guitarist, contemporary blues artist, and children's book author Keb' Mo' is a modern master of American roots music. B.B. King, Buddy Guy, the Dixie Chicks, Joe Cocker, Robert Palmer, and Tom Jones have all recorded his songs. He has collaborated with a host of artists, including Bonnie Raitt, Jackson Browne, Cassandra Wilson, Buddy Guy, Amy Grant, Solomon Burke, Little Milton, and many others. He has also been featured in TV shows and films. Keb' has received an honorary doctorate degree in music from Williams College.

Keb' is also a proud supporter of the Plastic Pollution Coalition and released the song "Don't Throw It Away" in support of its global mission to stop plastic pollution.

Plastic Pollution Coalition is a growing global alliance of more than 1,200 organizations, businesses, and thought leaders in 75 countries working toward a world free of plastic pollution and its toxic impact on humans, animals, waterways, the ocean, and the environment.

plastic**pollution**coalition

In an effort to improve our world and in collaboration with Trees for the Future (TREES), a tree will be planted for every book purchased. Our plant a tree partnership is a way for us to assist TREES in their efforts to heal the environment and alleviate poverty for smallholder farmers in impoverished countries. To learn more about TREES, visit http://trees.org/.